BEASTS
—OF—
OLYMPUS

To Rob, Brett, Giuseppe, and Hannah—
with many thanks for being on Team Olympus

GROSSET & DUNLAP
Penguin Young Readers Group
An Imprint of Penguin Random House LLC

The publisher does not have any control over and does not assume any responsibility
for author or third-party websites or their content.

Text copyright © 2015 by Lucy Coats. Illustrations copyright © 2015 by Brett Bean. All rights reserved.
Published by Grosset & Dunlap, an imprint of Penguin Random House LLC, 345 Hudson Street, New York,
New York 10014. GROSSET & DUNLAP is a trademark of Penguin Random House LLC.
Printed in the USA.

Library of Congress Cataloging-in-Publication Data is available.

ISBN 978-0-448-46196-0   10 9 8 7 6 5 4 3

BEASTS
—OF—
OLYMPUS

by Lucy Coats   art by Brett Bean

Dragon Healer

GROSSET & DUNLAP
An Imprint of Penguin Rand

CHAPTER 1

RIOT IN THE STABLES

Demon, son of the beast god, Pan, and proud new bearer of King Poseidon's Order of Ocean, shot up and out of the clear green waters of Melanie's spring.

"Urgh! Aggh! Pftha!" he spluttered, shaking his head wildly to get the liquid out of his ears as his lungs adjusted to the warm, sunny air of Olympus. He took a deep, clean-smelling breath and let out a sigh of relief. The air smelled of fragrant flowers and honey, just like it was supposed to. There was not a trace of stinky beast-poo odor, which meant that hopefully he wouldn't be turned into a pile of smoking Demon-shaped charcoal by a crowd of annoyed goddesses. Not today, anyway.

Melanie the naiad, who was sitting on a mossy rock and combing her long blue hair, gave him a nasty look as he struggled out onto dry land, dripping, and trailing his magic silver medicine box behind him. It was covered in great globs of slimy silver seaweed.

"Finished messing up my nice clean spring with that horrid sea stuff, have you?" she snarled angrily.

Demon picked a couple of flapping flatfish out of his tunic and threw them back into the water.

"Yes," he said, wondering why she sounded like a crazed Chimera. Melanie was normally nice to him. "I'm all finished, actually. Er, is anything wrong? You seem a little upset." Melanie frowned and waved a hand toward the Stables of the Gods.

"Well, of course there's something wrong. You've got to go and do something about those noisy beasts of yours, Demon. They've been bellowing and bawling ever since Hermes brought that nasty boy Autolykos up here. It's no wonder I'm upset. I haven't had a wink of sleep all week." She yawned loudly, showing two perfect rows of pearly white teeth. As his ears finally popped back to normal, Demon heard a terrible racket coming from the Stables of the Gods. Now he knew exactly what

Melanie meant. Without another word, he picked up his box and ran. What on earth was happening in there? It sounded as if every single beast was rioting and rumpusing out of control!

Inside the Stables, it was complete chaos. Almost every pen had a baaing, neighing, screeching, shrieking beast leaping up and down. A tall, dark-haired boy whirled around and around in the middle of the center aisle, waving a broom and banging on the bars.

"Leave me alone," he shouted. "Shut UP, you awful, noisy creatures!"

Demon dumped the silver box on the floor, pulled out his father's magical pipes, and blew a short, sharp blast. Immediately, there was silence.

"Who are YOU?" asked the boy, dropping his broom in mid-bang. "And how did you do that?"

"I'm Demon," said Demon. "Son of Pan and official stable boy to the gods. And you must be Autolykos. What in the name of Hades's handkerchiefs have you done to the poor things to make them act out like this?"

"Nothing," said Autolykos sulkily. "I've fed and cleaned the stupid creatures. What more do they want?"

"Huh!" said the griffin loudly to Demon, clacking its sharp beak against the bars of its pen. "'Nothing,' he says, the lousy, lying thief! He's only gone and stolen half the feathers from the winged horses' wings so they can't fly, AND he's upset Doris, AND he's dumped half the ambrosia cake down the poo chute!"

"Yes!" chorused the rest of the beasts. "He did!"

"Rotten robber!"

"Snackie stealer!"

"Feather pincher!"

"See?" said Autolykos. "Garble, garble, garble! On they go, whimpering and whining. I don't know how you put up with it."

"Stolen the winged horses' feathers, eh?" said Demon grimly, stalking toward him as the noise levels rose again. "Tipped the ambrosia cake down the poo chute? Upset my poor Hydra?"

A purple tide of rage was creeping up from his toes. Nobody was allowed to treat his beasts like this! NOBODY!

"H-h-h-how? W-w-what do you mean? I-I-I never . . ."

"Oh yes you did," said Demon, shouting to be heard over the racket. "What you hear as garble, I hear as words, so don't try to deny it."

"Oh, all RIGHT, then!" said Autolykos sullenly. "So what if I did? I only hit that idiot Hydra because it drooled all over the cake, and it was only a few stupid feathers I took, anyway, and—"

"And now my flying horses CAN'T FLY!" roared Demon. Even though Autolykos was bigger than him, Demon suddenly felt he had the strength of ten stable boys. He grabbed the boy by the scruff of the neck and ran him out of the Stables, past Melanie's spring, and all the way over to the Iris Express.

"Stop it! Leggo of me! Get off!" bawled Autolykos. But Demon was determined to get rid of him.

"One passenger for earth," he yelled, pulling handfuls of fluffy horse feathers out of Autolykos's tunic with his other hand as they went. "And don't bother too much with the seat belts!"

"HEY!" shouted Autolykos. "Give those back! I could have sold them for a FORTUNE! They're MINE!"

"Oh no they aren't!" said Demon, shoving him onto the transparent wisp of rainbow. "I would hang on tight if I were you," he added as the Iris Express gave an eye-watering lurch and whooshed downward. There was a sudden choked-off scream and some noisy retching, which trailed away into nothing. The Iris Express could be scary and sick-making if you had a weak stomach and no head for heights.

"Serves him right," muttered Demon, picking up all the scattered feathers from the grass where they'd fallen and smoothing them out carefully. He trotted back to the Stables, grumbling to himself and vowing never to go away again.

"Why can't the gods just leave me alone?" he said as he walked into the comforting musty, dusty, beasty smell of the place he now called home. "Every time one of them takes me away from my job, it all goes horribly wrong up here. First it's Hades with poor sneezing Cerberus, then Poseidon with his itchy Hippocamps." Demon sighed a huge sigh. When would he ever get five minutes' peace?

The racket died down to a quiet grumble as he walked into the Stables and went down the aisles, petting and stroking all his beasts and hearing their stories about how awful Autolykos had been to them. A big bubble of anger built up in his stomach as he rubbed poor Doris the Hydra's bruises. Why were people so awful to animals? He just didn't understand it.

"Oy! Pan's scrawny kid! Come over here and let me out," came a snarky voice from the griffin's pen, breaking into his thoughts. "I want a private word with you!"

Demon unlatched the pen and stalked out of the Stables, the griffin padding behind on its huge lion's feet.

"What now?" he said. "Spit it out. That wretched Autolykos left me a lot to do, in case you hadn't noticed."

"Aaah!" The griffin sighed, stretching its wings in the bright sunlight and flapping them to get the dust out. "That's better. I've missed being outside." It looked at Demon shrewdly from one of its fierce orange eyes. "Now, what was it I wanted to say? Ah, yes! I believe you owe me a little something, Pan's scrawny kid. A little something beginning with *M* and ending with *T*, with a tasty little *E* and *A* in the middle."

Demon marched over to it, standing on tiptoe until he was nose to sharp, pointy beak with the great beast. "No. I. Do. NOT!" he growled. "The deal was that you and the Nemean Lion had to look after the Stables properly while I was away." He gestured back through the doors at the mess of spoiled ambrosia, tipped-over poo barrows, wisps of golden sun hay, and fallen-over rakes that made the Stables look as if a small hurricane had blown through. "I don't call THAT properly!"

"It's not MY fault. Me and Lion were doing fine till Hermes brought that thieving oaf in," said the griffin sulkily. "I had the ambrosia cake all locked away from Doris and everything. The whole place was spick-and-span and shining till Hermes came along and started meddling. That's when it all started to go wrong—bratty boy Autolykos just didn't understand anything we said, and he didn't care about us, either. Not like you do. Doris wasn't the only one he hit with that horrible broom, you know, but Hermes put an anti-beast protection spell around him, so we couldn't get him back."

Demon sighed, all the anger draining out of him. "I'm sorry he treated you all so badly," he said, stroking the griffin's rough lion pelt. "I'm sure you did your best. I'll have a word with Hermes—see if he can't smuggle up a few juicy steaks from earth or something. Now, we'd better get back and start fixing this mess. As far as I can see, it's going to take all day to get it settled. But before I do any cleaning up, I must see if my box has something to stick the feathers back on the winged horses. They said they were desperate to fly again."

The griffin batted Demon with a paw, making him fall flat on his face. "Good to have you back, Pan's scrawny kid. And I'll hold you to your promise about the juicy you-know-whats. If I don't get something decent to eat soon, even your skinny carcass is going to start to look tasty!" A long pink tongue swiped his face. "Yum yum!" the griffin said, clacking its beak menacingly by his ear.

"Oh, shut up, Griffin," said Demon, scrambling to his feet and dusting off his already filthy tunic. "You know I'd give you terrible indigestion. Now, where's that box of mine?"

The magic silver medicine box was exactly where he'd left it, in the middle of the passage where he'd dropped it when he'd run into the Stables. He picked it up and went down the row of pens till he came to the winged-horse stalls. Oh, dear! They were a sorry sight. Their beautiful wings were half bald, their coats were dull, their tails were drooping, and even the little golden horns in the middle of their foreheads looked sad.

"Itchy-scratch?" said Keith, the boss horse, hopefully, presenting his left ear.

"Definitely," said Demon. "But later. First, I need to get these feathers of yours fixed."

CHAPTER 2

THE PATENTED PYRO-PROTECTION KIT

Demon was just peeling the bits of feather and icky-sticky stuff off his fingers after mending the horses' wings when the carved-head alarm on the back wall of the Stables started to squawk.

"Incoming! Incoming! Double-flaming incoming!" it yelled. "Deploy pyro-protection kit! Deploy pyro-protection kit!" Demon had no idea what was happening. What kind of beast did the head mean when it said "double-flaming incoming"? And what was a pyro-protection kit?

He looked around frantically.

"Where do I get a pyro-whatever kit?" he asked the griffin in a panicky voice as loud, angry moos and bellows came from the direction of the Iris Express.

"Hospital shed," said the griffin. "Third drawer on the left. Hurry up, Pan's scrawny kid. You haven't got much time before those things burn down the whole of Olympus. I'm off to fetch the Fire Officer." Flapping its wings frantically, the griffin took off.

Demon didn't know what kind of beast "those things" were, and he didn't have time to ask. Running faster than a speeding salamander, he raced over to the hospital shed, ripped open the third drawer on the left, and pulled out what looked like a floppy, silvery human body. It had a strange opening up the front, covered feet, and finger-shaped bits at the ends of the arms. Demon shook it out and turned it around. What was it? Was he supposed to wear it? If so, how did he get into it? He touched the small tag at the top of the opening. Was that a clue?

"Pull down on tag!" said a crackly voice. Demon jumped backward in fright. "Come on!" said the voice impatiently. "Hurry up!" So Demon pulled, fumbling slightly in his haste. The tag slid down smoothly, revealing two sets of sharp teeth on either side.

"Climb in," said the voice. "And welcome to Hephaestus's patented pyro-protection body kit. What is your fire situation level, please?"

"I don't know!" said Demon, hurriedly stepping into the kit's suit and pulling it up over his feet and legs. "But I need to get to the Iris Express, fast!" Immediately a hood flipped out and over his hair, and a clear mask sealed itself around his face as the tag shot upward, fastening the two sets of teeth together with a crunch.

"Pyro protection in place," said the suit. "You may now proceed safely to the danger zone. Please breathe normally." Demon was already running again as the rest of the silvery material molded itself tightly to his body. The angry bellows were getting louder, and there was an ominous cloud of smoke and sparks rising from above the Iris Express.

As Demon skidded to a halt, he saw several things all at once. First, there were several trees on fire, their big bunches of silvery-golden fruit bursting with big squelchy pops in the heat. Then there was the grass, which had huge, steaming scorch marks running across it.

The main problem was obvious. Two enormous bulls with golden rings in their noses were roaring and rampaging about, snorting and spurting giant streams of fire out of their nostrils. Everything they touched burst into flames. Their brass hooves churned and pawed the ground, and their bodies were covered with deep cuts that bled bright red, smoking blood. Trusting that the pyro-protection kit would keep him safe, Demon darted forward through a wall of fire and grabbed the two nose rings. A gust of flame swept over him, but all he felt was a warm bath of sunlight.

"Whoa!" he shouted. "Calm down! I can fix your wounds, but you have to stop setting stuff on fire!" The two bulls took no notice. They both tossed their heads into the air at the same time, making Demon lose his grip and sending him flying, just missing a sharp horn by a whisker. "Oof!" he gasped as he landed flat on his back and rolled sideways into a patch of burning grass to dodge the flailing hooves. He reached for his Pan pipes, but they were trapped inside the pyro-protection kit.

"Get this thing off me! I need my pipes! Or a pocket?" he yelled, tearing helplessly at the shiny silver material. Immediately a bulge formed by his right hand.

"Pocket now operational," said the suit.

As he grabbed the pipes and scrabbled them up to his mouth, the mask opened just enough for him to blow a short trill of notes. But for the very first time, his dad's magical present failed him, and the beasts just kept on rampaging. By now, the fire was spreading everywhere, and shrieking nymphs were jumping out of trees and flowers and running toward the shining white buildings where the gods and goddesses lived. Demon blew the pipes again and again in a hundred different ways, trying to calm down the frantic, wounded beasts, but nothing worked. Just as he'd been tossed into the fires for about the twenty-fourth time, a thunderous shout came from behind him.

"Khalko! Kafto! Cease and desist, you wretched beasts!" It was the smith god, Hephaestus, Fire Officer of Olympus, with a crowd of automaton robots behind him. He walked through the flames, reached out two long, sooty arms, and seized both bulls by the tips of their horns. Then he clashed their heads together and kicked their brass hooves out from underneath them so that they crashed to the ground, their fire draining away to a dribble.

"Thanks, Heffy," Demon groaned through his mask, rubbing his bruises as he got to his feet.

"No time for that," said the smith god. "Go and fetch a double dose of saffron-crocus juice—the red kind—and bring it back here as quick as you can while I put out these fires. It's the only thing that will save my bulls." Demon didn't argue. He limped as quickly as he could back to the hospital shed, grabbed the little glass bottle of red liquid from his stores, and limped back again. By the time he got there, Hephaestus had set five of his automaton robots to digging a firebreak, and was flailing at the remaining flames with a bristly fire broom in each hand. Khalko and Kafto were still lying on the ground, their terrible wounds smoking and bleeding onto the scorched earth, but now their eyes were closed and the flames had died completely. Demon kneeled down beside the bulls, his bruises forgotten. He hated to see any beast like this.

"Who did this to you?" he asked angrily. "Was it that wretched Heracles again?" But the bulls didn't reply.

"Just treat their wounds with the saffron juice," Hephaestus shouted as he batted out a spray of sparks. "They'll be fine if you do that. I designed it especially for them!" Wondering what the smith god meant, Demon smoothed a drop of the medicine into every wound, staining the fingertips of the pyro-protection kit a bright red. Hephaestus had to give him a hand with turning each of the huge bodies over so he could do both sides. It took him a long time, but by the time he had finished, the wounds had all stopped smoking and were closing up nicely.

"What happened?" Demon asked again, when the bulls opened their eyes and began to stir.

"Dragon men!" Khalko coughed.

"Jason!" Kafto coughed, letting out a small spurt of flame.

"I think I'd better get you both into a nice, safe, fireproof pen beside the Cretan Bull," Demon said. "Then you can tell me all about it."

"Off you go," said Hephaestus. "We'll finish up here. Good job, Pandemonius! Come and tell me how they are later." As Demon led the two bulls off toward the special pens at the back of the Stables, he could hear Hephaestus pestering some dryads into healing the trees and grass, and telling a gang of nymphs to polish the soot off all the flowers. Soon Olympus would be back to its normal, beautiful self.

"Make yourselves comfortable," he said, swinging open the big stone doors of the pen for the bulls to enter. "I'll just go and fetch you some nice ambrosia cake to eat."

"All fixed, Pan's scrawny kid?" asked the griffin as Demon went outside again, flapping down to meet him from its lookout perch on the roof. "Everything under control? Any chance of you wearing normal clothes again anytime soon? You look like a squeegee stick insect in that pyro thing."

Demon looked down at himself. It was true. His legs did look long and spindly, encased in tight-fitting silver. But he wasn't complaining. The pyro-protection kit had saved him from being frazzled to a crisp.

"You're just jealous you can't have one, Griffin,"
he said, "but I suppose you're right. I'd better take it
off now." At once, the pyro-protection kit's crackly
voice sounded in his ear.

"Safety check. Please report on status of fire
situation."

"All clear," said Demon. "I'm well away from it now."
Immediately, the suit began to loosen around him.

"Initiating undressing process," it said as the
hood and mask retracted. "Pull tag in a downward
direction and step out." It wasn't as easy as it
sounded, but Demon eventually struggled out of
the suit and bundled it untidily on top of a bale of
sun hay outside the Stables.

"I'll sort you out later," he said.

"All folding assistance gratefully received,"
said the suit. "Thank you for your valued custom.
Hephaestus's patented pyro-protection body kit is
here to serve all your flaming emergencies."

CHAPTER 3
THE BRASS BULLS

Once they'd settled down and were munching comfortably, the bulls told him their story.

"There was this hero, see?" said Khalko. Demon rolled his eyes. Heroes were mostly nothing but beast-battering bullies, as far as he was concerned.

"Yeah. Jason, he was called," said Kafto. "He beat us up and made us plow a great big muddy field, and then he sowed all these teeth in it."

"Dragon's teeth, he called them," said Khalko.

"Only they didn't grow dragons, they grew dragon men."

"Stone ones, with axes and spears and swords," said Kafto. "They sprang up out of nowhere and started fighting Jason."

"And fighting us, too," said Khalko. "They were running around stabbing anything that moved. That's where we got all those nasty wounds."

"What happened then?" asked Demon.

"Well, we don't really remember much after

that, because we went a bit crazy," said Kafto. "But I think I heard a girl yelling about putting a dragon to sleep and telling Jason to hurry."

"Yeah. And I saw Jason climbing up a tree with a big furry gold bundle hanging on it," said Khalko. "Then we must have somehow got dead in the earthly realms and sent up here."

"Yes," said Demon. "That's what usually happens to you poor immortal beasts. And then I have to patch you up. Never mind, you'll be safe now. I'll bring you some more cake when you've finished that—you need building up after what you've been through." There was a sudden bellow and a spray of sparks from the pen next door. Demon poked his head over the wall.

"All right, all right," he said to the Cretan Bull next door. "You can have some, too. Greedy beast! Maybe while you're waiting, you can tell these two how horrible Heracles put out your fire."

Demon hurried back with the cake and tipped it into the mangers. Soon the three bulls were mooing and munching contentedly together. Then he grabbed a broom and began to tidy up the mess that Autolykos had left. It took him the rest of the day and most of the evening. By the time he'd eaten his own supper of fresh ambrosia cake, he was exhausted. He climbed the stairs to his little loft room above the Stables and flopped down on the bed. Pulling his spider-silk blanket over him, he prayed to Zeus that no more emergencies happened in the night. He had a bad feeling that he hadn't heard the last of Jason's misdoings.

The next morning, though, everything seemed as if it was back to normal. Demon trotted about the Stables, barrowing poo, filling mangers, sweeping, and chatting with the beasts.

"I missed you all," he said to Doris, who was

happily following him around. Its nine mouths were full of brooms and buckets. "Poseidon's kingdom was interesting, and I'm sad not to have Eunice around, but I like being up here better."

"Snackies?" the huge green Hydra asked hopefully, dropping a bucket on his toes.

Demon danced around on one foot. "Later," he said, rubbing his bruised toes. "I'll have to go and ask the kitchen fauns to deliver some more supplies. Autolykos was right about one thing—you did drool on most of it." He patted Doris's green flanks. "It's a shame you didn't drown HIM in drool, really!"

After Demon had stacked the ambrosia cake neatly, he made his way to Hephaestus's workshop under the mountain. Loud bangs and crashes came from within, and he cautiously put his head inside, remembering the time when he'd made the mistake of entering when the forge was fired up in dragon mode. But the warning slate had no pictures of fearsome dragons or skulls and crossbones on it, so he went inside. Hephaestus was hammering away at an enormous silver-and-gold bowl, nearly big enough to take a bath in.

"What's that for?" asked Demon.

"Zeus wants it to give to some king he favors down on earth," said Hephaestus, putting down his hammer and reaching for a smaller silver one. He began tapping away on the inside of the bowl, and under his clever fingers a picture of Zeus and his thunderbolts began to emerge on the outside. "I'm putting a little magic in it so that whatever food or drink is put in it will never run out. Now, how are those bulls of mine, young Pandemonius?"

"I meant to ask you about that," Demon said. "What do you mean, *your* bulls?"

"Yes, yes," said the god testily. "My bulls. Khalko and Kafto. I made them, see? They're a bit like my automatons, half full of brass and gizmos inside. Gave them to the King of Colchis as a gift years ago. He's a real piece of work, but he did me a favor once."

"Well, he didn't take very good care of them, did he, lending them to that horrible Jason person? I think they should stay up here now—I'll look after them much better than he did." Then Demon frowned, remembering something. "I suppose if they're sort of robots, that was why they didn't respond to my dad's pipes—but then how come they were bleeding all over the place?"

"Ah! That's the ingenious part," said Hephaestus, looking very pleased with himself. "I wanted to make them as real as possible, so I invented a mixture that looked like blood to put inside them. That red crocus juice is the main ingredient, which is why they needed it to make them better." He paused to wipe his brow with one grimy hand.

"By the way, young Pandemonius, I hope you've sorted out all that racket that was coming from the Stables when you were off looking after Poseidon's fish-beasts. I meant to find out what was going on, but I've been busy. Which reminds me, you'd better get out of here—I've got a big order of armor from Ares to do next, and that'll mean putting the forge in dragon mode."

Demon didn't need telling twice. One encounter with the dragon forge was quite enough for anyone! As he trotted back to the Stables, humming happily to himself, he heard a flap-flapping of wings above him.

"Oy! Pan's scrawny kid!" called the griffin, swooping down and landing in front of him with a puff of dust. "You'd better get inside quick. There's some girl in there, and she wants to see you."

"Does she have aquamarine-y eyes and dark green hair?" he asked, beginning to run. Maybe it was his Nereid friend Eunice, come to visit him from Poseidon's realm, he thought. Maybe she had a problem with the Hippocamps again. He hoped it was her—he was really missing Eunice's company. He'd liked having a friend his own age to talk to. The griffin snorted through its beak.

"Not exactly. You'll see. And I'd hurry if I were you. She doesn't look too happy."

Demon saw, all right, as soon as he skidded to a halt in front of her. The girl had long, shiny black hair that coiled and moved by itself, bright snake-green eyes, and sharp, pointy fingernails, which were clutching at her long white silk robes. She was older than Eunice, and she definitely wasn't a goddess; Demon knew that at once. She wasn't nearly scary enough. She wasn't a naiad or a dryad or a nymph, either. The word that wormed its way into Demon's mind was . . . *witch*. She had a kind of dry, crackly, magicky smell about her.

"Er . . . what can I do for you, ma'am?" he said cautiously. It didn't hurt to be polite to someone who might have magic powers. You never knew what they might turn you into.

"Are you Pandemonius, the stable boy?" she asked. Demon nodded. "Then you're the one I need," she said, sounding relieved. "Come with me."

Demon's mind was racing as he followed her beckoning finger out the back door of the Stables and toward the poo chute, where the hundred-armed monsters roared and raged below. There was a light chariot parked beside the poo pile, with two small winged creatures yoked to it. They had long, sinuous bodies spotted with black and gold, bright orange crests on their heads, and tiny short legs with clawed feet. They were also lying down in their traces and panting with exhaustion.

"What in the name of Ares's armor are those?" he exclaimed.

"SHHH!" his companion hissed in a panicky voice, clutching his arm tightly with her sharp nails. "Don't mention HIM! He might find me! I'm not supposed to be here at all!" Demon wrenched his arm out of her grip. Witch or not, he wanted to know what was going on.

"I think you'd better tell me just who you are and why I should do you a favor," he said sternly. "I don't mind helping your beasts, but I'm not getting in trouble with the gods again. I've had quite enough of that, thank you very much!" The witch-girl immediately collapsed to her knees, sobbing. Demon felt terrible. He hadn't meant to make her cry.

"Come on," he said, helping her up and taking her over to a nearby boulder. "Sit down here." He fumbled in his tunic and pulled out a grubby handkerchief, which he handed to her. She looked at it doubtfully before taking it and blowing her nose loudly.

"I-I'm P-Princess M-Medea," she said. "I'm in dreadful trouble with A-A . . . er . . . the god of war for using my powers to help my boyfriend steal something from the god's sacred grove, and now he's threatened to k-kill me, so I have to go into hiding. O-only I can't take my flying dragons with me—everyone knows they're mine, and they'd give me away. My grandfather told me you were good with beasts, so I thought I'd bring them to you and see if you'd look after them. I was just going to leave them for you to find, but flying all the way up here has exhausted them, and now I'm worried they're going to d-die." As she began to sob again, Demon got up to look at the two small beasts. It had to be said, they didn't look too good.

"Wait here," Demon said, wondering who her grandfather was and how he knew that Demon was good with beasts. "I'll just go and fetch my medicine box."

"Oh, please do hurry," said Princess Medea. "I'm not sure they can last much longer."

CHAPTER 4

A DAY FULL OF DRAGONS

Demon dumped the box beside the two dragons and opened its lid. "I need something to wake up these poor beasts, please, box," he said as Princess Medea hovered anxiously by his shoulder. "I think they're just tired out, but could you have a look?"

The magic box began to glow blue, and strange symbols ran over its silver sides. Two long tubes, each with a silver disc on the end, uncoiled and shot out from its top, clamping onto the dragons' chests. After a few seconds, they retracted with a snap.

"Extreme exantlisis detected," said the box in its metallic warble. "Remove remedy from medicine port and reboot subjects via mouth." There was a small click, and a bottle of bright orange liquid appeared, together with a silver spoon.

"What did all that mean?" asked Princess Medea. "I didn't understand a word of it." Demon sighed. As usual, the box was using its stupid cryptic language.

"Don't worry about it," he said. "It's just saying they're completely exhausted. The box always talks like that. I think Hephaestus designed it to be annoying on purpose, but it does always come up with the right medicine in the end." He poured out a large spoonful of the orange liquid and carefully dribbled it into the nearer dragon's mouth. It had a strange fringed lip, which lifted up to reveal two rows of needle-sharp teeth. As he was finishing with the second dragon's dose, the first one opened its eyes, lunged sideways, and bit his bottom. Hard. It burned like acid.

"Ouch!" he yelled, leaping backward and clutching himself as Offy and Yukus, the two snakes who made up his magical healing necklace, raced down his back toward the wound.

"Bad dragon," scolded Princess Medea. "Don't bite the nice stable boy. He's going to look after you while I'm away." She looked at Demon. "I must go before I'm caught up here by you-know-who," she said. "Take care of them, won't you?" Demon nodded as she took a vial out of her robe and tipped a drop onto her tongue.

"Ugh!" she said, and her body started to fade into a thin purple mist. "Disgusting stuff. No wonder my Jason didn't like taking it."

"Wait!" shouted Demon. "What do you mean, *your* Jason?" But it was too late. She had disappeared in a puff of smoke. What did Princess

Medea have to do with the hero who'd hurt Hephaestus's bulls?

The two dragons were writhing and thrashing in their harness by now, and it took Demon a little while to get them calmed down and untangled. He had some questions for them about their mistress, but first he had to find out what kind of dragons they were, and find them a pen to live in.

"Are you fire-breathers?" he asked, wondering where it was best to put them, as they waddled toward the Stables on their short, stumpy legs.

"No, we're poison-spitters," said one.

"And biters," said the other, baring its teeth. "Want me to show you how well I bite again?"

"Um, no, thanks," said Demon. "I'm good. I'll put you next to the giant scorpion, then. Feel free to spit at him—he won't even notice."

But just as Demon had settled his charges into their new home, the air in the Stables darkened and became colder. A smell of unwashed bodies and old blood wafted into his nostrils, and he began to hear the sound of tramping feet.

"Oh no!" he whispered as two lines of fully armored soldiers marched into the Stables, each with the sign of a bloody dagger on his breastplate. Demon knew the sound of an approaching god when he heard it.

"Halt! About-face! Present arms!" shouted one of them. With a metallic clatter, the soldiers turned to face each other, making an alleyway of crossed spears. Demon dropped to his knees and bowed his head as a gigantic figure in shining golden armor strode toward him. He didn't even have to lift his head to look. He knew exactly who had come to visit by the pair of gold-studded military-looking sandals that stopped right under his nose. It was Ares, god of war, accompanied by his godly bodyguards.

There was a rasp of metal, and Demon felt the tip of an unsheathed sword pressing under his chin to make him look up. He began to shake but quickly stopped when he felt a bead of blood trickle down his throat. Ares gazed down at him with cold eyes the color of a stormy sky.

"So, son of Pan," said the god in an unexpectedly high voice, which had a faint air of battle and screaming behind it. "We meet at last! I've heard so much about you. Quite the little healer, aren't you?" He lowered his sword and bent down, lifting Demon up by the front of his tunic and peering down to inspect the small cut he'd made. "Ah! Blood! How delightful. Nothing wrong with a little red blood, is there, boys?" He turned to look at his soldiers.

"No, sir! Nothing, sir!" shouted the godly bodyguards, beating their armored fists against their chests. Ares waved a hand at them, and they

snapped back to silent attention. Demon felt
a bit sick.

"You will come with me, stable boy," said Ares.
"I have a beast of mine I wish you to attend to.
Bring him." Without another word, he flung Demon
at one of the godly bodyguards and marched out.
The godly bodyguard caught him, set Demon down
amidst the others, and fell into formation behind
their master.

"Hut! Hut! Hut! One, two! One, two! One, two!"
they yelled in unison, pushing him along.

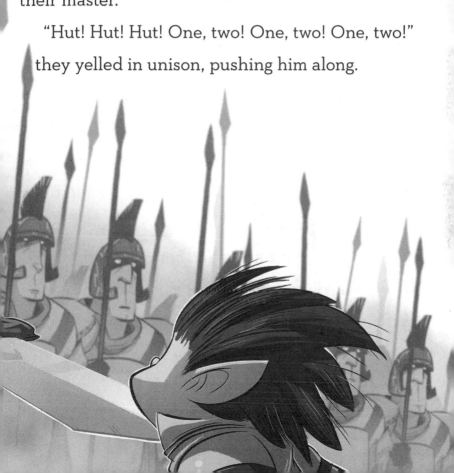

By the time he'd been marched through Olympus at what seemed like a million miles an hour, then thrown into the back of a war chariot that had four fiery horses harnessed to it, Demon was far too scared and winded to do anything other than lie there, trembling in every limb. He could feel Offy and Yukus mending the cut Ares had made—maybe they'd help him heal whatever beast it was that Ares wanted him to see to. If he survived that long. All he knew about Ares from listening to the nymphs gossip was that he was the cruelest of all the gods and that he worked with his sister, Eris, to sow hatred and enmity between the peoples down on earth. As the war chariot plunged downward, Demon rattled and smashed against the sides, trying desperately to hang on to something— anything—with his fingernails. Ares's whip cracked and snapped over the horses' heads as the god shouted for them to go faster.

"Pleasedon'tletmefalloutpleasedon'tletmefallout!"
Demon muttered over and over again, keeping his
eyes tightly shut as his fingers finally found a strap
and clung to it for dear life. If he was going to crash
to earth, he didn't want to see how far down it was.
There was a loud thump and bump as the chariot
wheels hit something hard, and Demon was jolted
right out of the back. He had barely started to
scream when all the breath was knocked out of him
as he landed suddenly on a bumpy surface, rolled
once, and came to a wheezing halt.

"You're late, brother," said a peevish voice. "And
who's this piece of worthless junk you've brought
with you?" A toe poked at Demon's heaving ribs,
and he opened his eyes to see a hard-faced goddess
looking down at him. She had short, greasy black
hair, a permanent sneer twisting her thin, bitten
lips, and small, angry eyes. "Is this what Zeus calls a
stable boy? He looks more like a squashed beetle to

me! And he smells like a dirty pigpen!" She turned away, looking disgusted, and stomped up a nearby hill, picking at a scab with one ragged nail.

"Stop lying there!" Ares screamed at him, waving his sword threateningly and jumping out of the chariot. "There's work to do! Get up and attend to my dragon at once, or I'll chop your legs into mincemeat and make you run around the parade ground for a century!" Demon scrambled up immediately, shaking with fear. Having his legs chopped into mincemeat might just be an even worse punishment than being turned into a little heap of Demon-shaped charcoal. And it would certainly hurt more.

"Y-y-yes, Your M-m-m-military M-m-mightiness," he whimpered, looking around him frantically. Ares strode off to join Eris and immediately started arguing loudly with her about who'd killed the most soldiers in the last war they'd started. Where was

the dragon? Finally, he spotted it a ways off, lying
under a thicket of bushes in the middle of a grove
of trees that were covered in golden leaves. Its
huge, flame-red, serpentine body lay very still, with
just a dying trickle of smoke coming from its jaws.
Demon began to run toward it.

Between him and the dragon was a muddy
plowed field with what looked like gray rocks lying
all over it. As he got closer, though, Demon saw that
they weren't rocks at all. They were bits of bodies.
Stony arms and legs lay scattered around like long,

gray boulders, with heads and torsos piled up in heaps. He had to slow down to avoid tripping over them. Some of the arms held spears and swords in their hands. What kind of battle left stone bodies behind? Then Demon saw a patch of steaming red blood and a large bronze plow tipped over on its side. Suddenly he remembered the story Khalko and Kafto had told him.

"Jason!" he whispered. "These must be all the dragon-teeth soldiers he killed." He started to run again, leaping over the scattered stone limbs like a deer. What if Jason had fatally wounded the dragon, too? What if Demon couldn't mend it? He thought about Ares and minced legs, and ran even faster.

CHAPTER 5

THE COLCHIAN DRAGON

The small trickle of smoke had died to almost
nothing when Demon finally reached the grove
of golden trees. He flung himself underneath the
thicket where the dragon lay and started to run his
hands over its body, looking for wounds. Its rough,
scaly hide felt pleasantly warm to the touch, but he
couldn't find anything wrong with it on the outside.
He shook its shoulder, making its mane of spikes
rattle.

"Wake up," he begged. "Oh, please wake up,

Dragon!" The dragon's eyelid twitched once.

"Go 'way!" it groaned, and its coils moved as it tried to pull itself into a tight ball. "I'm not here. You can't see me!"

"Of course I can see you," Demon said. "You're right in front of me!"

"Am not," it said. And it wrapped its tail around its head.

"What's wrong?" Demon asked. "Ares sent me to help you, but I can't unless you tell me where it hurts."

"Lalalalalalalalalala!" said the dragon, ignoring him and stuffing its claws in its ears. "Lalalalalalalalalala!"

"Oh, for Zeus's sake!" said Demon, exasperated. "There's nothing the matter with you. I'm going to go back to the chariot and tell Ares you're fine. You're just in a stupid sulk about something." As Demon turned to leave, a long red tail whipped out and trapped him within a tight coil of dragon. The coil began to squeeze.

"Am. Not. Sulking," said a grumpy-sounding voice by his ear. Demon could hardly breathe, what with the squeezing and the hot, sulfurous fumes coming from the dragon's mouth. His ribs began to crack and pop.

"All right, all right," Demon said breathlessly. "You're not sulking. I'm sorry. Just . . . just let me go, and tell me what IS wrong. I-I have to give Ares some sort of answer, or he . . . he'll chop my legs into mincemeat." Demon was panting each word out one at a time now, almost unable to breathe. The squeezing eased slightly, just as he felt something hot dripping onto his shoulder. Wriggling around in the coil that was still holding him, he managed to get a look at the dragon's head. Bright orange tears were streaming from its flame-like eyes, and as they hit the air, they hardened

into shining drops and fell to the ground with a tiny plink.

"Wow! Fire jewels!" he said, looking at the sparkling crystals. "That's amazing! I've never seen anything like them." He got his hand free and stroked the dragon's short, stubby horns. "Come on, I'm only Demon the stable boy. I'm your friend. You're safe with me. Tell me what happened to you." The dragon sighed, letting out another blast of sulfurous breath.

"Can't. Too ashamed," it mumbled, letting go of Demon and wrapping its tail around its head again. "Just kill me now and get it over with." Demon was outraged.

"Kill you?" he yelped. Then he clapped his hand over his mouth in case Ares heard. Lowering his voice, he went on, "I've never killed a beast in my life, and I don't intend to start now. Anyway, you're immortal. You can't be killed. Why are you so ashamed? Did that beastly Jason do something awful to you?" But before the dragon could reply, there was a shout from across the stony battlefield.

"What's taking you so long, stable boy? I'll give you ten seconds to get that dragon of mine up and running, otherwise it's minced legs for you—and maybe minced arms, as well! *Ten . . . nine . . . eight . . .*"

"Please, Dragon," Demon begged again. "Just get up and come back to Olympus with me. We can sort everything out there, and I'll find you a lovely, comfortable pen to stay in. If you don't, I-I-I'm g-going t-to b-be . . ." He was shaking so much, he couldn't finish the sentence.

"*Seven . . . six . . . five . . .*"

"Oh, fine," grumbled the dragon, uncurling itself and slithering over the stones toward the god of war. Demon began to run beside it. "But I don't like it up there, you know. It's a hateful place. And the other beasts are always nasty to me!"

"*Four . . . three . . . two . . .*" Just before Ares reached *one*, Demon and the dragon slid to a stop in front of him. Thinking fast, Demon kneeled immediately. He didn't know what was wrong, so he'd have to lie.

"I-I've examined your dragon, Your M-martial M-magnificence, a-a-and it . . . it's very sick. I-I think i-it may have been poisoned by Jason. I-i-it'll need a proper checkup in the Stables before I can make a r-real d-diagnosis," Demon panted. The dragon moaned loudly and coiled itself into a tight ball again.

"Sounds like you've got a great big, fat case of cowardice here, Ares," sneered Eris. "That overgrown snake with legs doesn't look very poisoned to me." She peered down at it malevolently. "Does the poor ickle-wickle dragon need to run away up to Olympus for an ickle-wickle vacation then?" she asked in a horrible babyish voice. Then she turned to face her brother, hands on her skinny hips. "I say stick it with your sword and get rid of it! It's no use to you like this!"

Ares drew his sword, and Demon tensed, ready to throw himself in front of the dragon. He couldn't allow it to be hurt, even if it meant being stabbed in the heart by the god himself. But instead of sticking the dragon, Ares whipped the sword sideways, and in a flash he had it held to his sister's throat.

"No one calls my sacred dragon a coward!" he snarled. "And I wouldn't put it past that worthless runt Hera favors to have poisoned him, either. He had that witch-princess Medea's help, and she's famous for her vile brews!" He turned to glower down at Demon. "I've got a nice little war in Thessaly I've got to go and stir up. Get this beast back to Olympus and have it fit and ready to report for duty by the time I get back, or . . ." He twitched his sword in a suggestive chopping motion, which made Demon's legs twitch with fear. "Come on, Eris," he yelled, jumping into his chariot. "Time to shed a lake of blood!"

"Oh, goody! What fun!" she squealed, leaping in beside him. "I feel like a nice, noisy battle with lots of shrieking and screaming! Let's ask Alecto and her Furies if they want to join in, too!" With a crack of the whip, the four fiery horses reared and raced up into the air.

What a horrible pair, thought Demon as the two deities disappeared from sight. But he didn't say it out loud, just in case they were listening.

"Have they gone?" asked the dragon weakly, raising its head.

"Yes, thank Hermes, they have," said Demon. "And now I have to find a way of getting you back to Olympus." He chewed on a thumbnail, thinking. Wounded beasts normally arrived at the Stables via the Iris Express. But who called it for them? He'd never thought to ask. If it was the god or goddess who looked after them, then he was in trouble. Ares had gone, and there were no other gods around.

"Can you call the Iris Express?" he asked the dragon hopefully.

"Oh no!" it moaned. "I'm not summoning that thing. I'll fall through it. It's not safe."

"That's what I thought when I first went on it," said Demon soothingly. "But it's fine, really. It's brought me all sorts of sick beasts, and never dropped one. Do you really know how to call it? It would be a big help if you could."

"If I really must." The dragon sighed. "But I'll warn you, you'll regret it if you take me up there." Just then a long *paaaaarrrppp* sounded from its nether regions. The gassy stench of rotten eggs and old socks almost knocked Demon over.

"Phew!" he said, fanning a hand in front of his

face. "We'll definitely have to find something to cure *that*! You're worse than the Cattle of the Sun on ambrosia!"

"I shall ignore that, as you have ignored my warning," said the dragon huffily. Then it cleared its throat with a small explosion of gray smoke. "Iris Express for beast and boy! Olympus bound!" Nothing happened.

"Perhaps you need to say it a bit louder," Demon suggested, breathing in shallowly through his mouth and resisting the temptation to hold his nose. The smell had now become truly dreadful.

"IRIS EXPRESS FOR BEAST AND BOY! OLYMPUS BOUND!" roared the dragon, sparks coming out of its mouth and igniting the gas from its bottom with a loud *WHUMP!* Demon jumped back, beating out the small flames that were about to set fire to his tunic. He could smell frizzling hair, too, but just as he was about to reach his spare

hand up to bat at it, a shower of
rain sprinkled on him, soaking him
to the skin. Shaking the water out of his
eyes, and steaming slightly, he saw a blaze of
rainbow light erupt from the sky above.

"Celestial fire extinguisher activated," said a
familiar tinkly voice. "Please ensure all flames
are out before boarding." The Iris Express had
arrived!

Demon was pretty sure
he wasn't alight anymore,
but he ran his
hands over himself
just in case
before coaxing
the dragon on
board the wisp of
nothingness.

"My dragon friend

here is a very nervous traveler," he said. "Do you think you could provide your usual arrangement to tie us both on, please?"

Immediately, rainbow-colored ropes looped themselves around both Demon and the dragon.

"Please hold on tightly for takeoff," said Iris as she whooshed off into the heavens.

Braaaaammmpppp! went the dragon's bottom again. Demon quickly sucked in a deep lungful of clean air before the smell hit. But he couldn't hold his breath forever. Choking and spluttering as the Iris Express landed, he stumbled out into the warm air of Olympus with the dragon trailing reluctantly behind him.

CHAPTER 6

STINKY OLYMPUS AGAIN

"Pooh!" said a passing nymph as they went by her. "What's that stink? You don't want the goddesses smelling *that!*"

"See!" muttered the dragon, his horns beginning to droop. "It's started already. They all hate me!"

"Don't be silly," said Demon. "Nobody hates you. And we'll have your . . . uh . . . little problem fixed in no time. Just wait till I find my magic healing box. It'll sort you out. Now come on, follow me. Let's get you into one of the special dragon pens." He trotted off in the direction of the Stables, hoping that there would be no more gassy blasts on the way there. The nymph was right. If the goddesses got even one whiff of the dragon's stench near their laundry, they'd turn Demon into a pile of charcoal dust quicker than he could say "stinky butt." The dragon heaved its heavy red coils behind him, leaving a trail of flattened grass behind it.

"Oy! Pan's scrawny kid!" hissed the griffin, stalking up behind him on its lion's feet. "Where's that meat you promised me? I'm starving!" It clacked its beak hungrily near his ear.

"Not now, Griffin," Demon said impatiently. "Can't you see I'm busy? I told you I'd ask Hermes, and I will. But at the moment . . . well . . . as you can see, we've got a new beast in the Stables, and I've got to take care of it right away."

"Huh!" said the griffin, lashing its tail. "Dragon, isn't it? I remember you. Didn't old Soldier Sandals drag you off to one of his sacred groves to guard something? What was it? I forget now."

"The Golden Fleece," muttered the dragon, looking behind it shiftily. "And don't call my boss that—he's got ears everywhere, you know." Sneering in its usual manner, the griffin turned around, flapped its wings once, and flew off to its perch on the roof. Demon led the dragon toward the very back of the Stables, pulled open the heavy flameproof doors, and took it into the deepest cave of all. He crossed his fingers and hoped that the rock would keep any smells from leaking out.

"You have a nice lie-down and close your eyes, Dragon," he said. "I'll just go and fetch my box, and then you can have something to eat." But just as he was about to walk away, the dragon looped him with its tail again, preventing him from leaving.

"Please don't go!" it said.

"Why not?" Demon asked. "Don't you want me

to try to make you better?"

"Yes," said the dragon. Its voice sounded sad, so Demon stroked its horns gently. "B-but I need to tell someone what happened down there, or I'll burst!" As if to back up its words, it let a tiny *paaarp* out of its bottom. Demon buried his nose in its warm scales, trying not very successfully to block out the resulting stink as the dragon began its tale.

"I guarded the Grove of the Golden Fleece in Colchis for years, never sleeping, always on watch. They called me Old Observant Eyes, and I was proud of the trust Ares had placed in me, his very own dragon. I even gave up my teeth willingly to his friend King Aeetes because I knew that they would grow strong soldiers to help me defend my master's Grove."

"Oh!" said Demon, interrupting. "So they were *your* teeth Jason sowed in that field?"

"Yes, yes," said the dragon a little testily. "I'm

getting to that bit. Now don't interrupt again, or I shall squeeze you." Demon shut his mouth quickly. His ribs still ached from the last squeezing the dragon had given him.

"I had one friend in the world," the dragon went on. "Or I thought I did. The witch-princess Medea, King Aeetes's daughter, used to come and visit me every day. She was the one who harvested my teeth once a year, and she did it so gently that I never even felt them go. She used to polish my scales with a soft cloth and sing to me. Then, last week, a ship arrived on the shores of Colchis. A ship full of heroes. I knew they had come to steal the Golden Fleece, because Medea had told me so. She said that their leader, Jason, was very cunning, and asked me to stay particularly alert, to watch as I'd never watched before. She said that she would bring me some of her special juniper potion to put on my eyelids so that I

would be able to see in all directions." The dragon's voice sounded absolutely miserable now.

"It was a trick. I allowed her to paint the potion on my eyelids, and I waited for it to work. But instead of being able to see in all directions, my eyes closed, and I fell into a trance. I, the unsleeping, ever-awake Colchian Dragon, failed my master. In my dreams, I saw Jason as Medea smeared him with an ointment of invincibility. I saw how he mastered Khalko and Kafto. I saw him plant my teeth and fight the stone warriors who rose up from the ground. I felt him climb over my sleeping body and cut down the Golden Fleece with his sword. I saw him run to his ship, with Medea laughing beside him, as she made them both invisible to her father and his soldiers."

By now, the hot tears were running from the dragon's eyes again, and fire jewels were plinking and pinging all over the rocky floor of the cave.

"I-I was so ashamed to have f-failed that I wanted to disappear," it sobbed. "I s-still do! I don't d-d-deserve any k-kindness, and besides, I-I've been banished from Olympus. Ares must have forgotten that when he l-let you bring me up here. Last time, the goddesses said that they'd send me down to Tartarus to live with the hundred-armed monsters if I ever came here again, b-because I'm s-such a s-smelly beast." It let out another tiny *toot* and the cave filled with more of its noxious stink.

"S-see!" it wailed. "This is what happens when I get upset! No one can cure me of it! Just leave me alone! I *deserve* to go to Tartarus!" It unlooped itself from around Demon's body and coiled itself into a hiccuping dragon ball of misery.

Demon didn't know what to do. He wanted to comfort it, but he was about to choke from trying not to breathe.

"I'll be back soon with my box," he said. "Try

not to worry—I'm sure we'll be able to find a cure somehow. And I won't let anyone send you to Tartarus."

As soon as he got back into the main Stables, there was a tremendous clamor.

"Food!" bellowed the three fiery bulls.

"Food!" whinnied the winged horses.

"Food!" roared the Nemean Lion.

BANG! went the giant scorpion's stinger against the pen door.

"Snackies!" Doris the Hydra drooled, clattering its brooms and buckets.

"All right! All right!" yelled Demon. "I'm coming!" He fed all his charges as quickly as he could, then went to fetch the box from the hospital shed. Running his eyes over the shelves of medicinal herbs and plants, he spotted a bunch of peppermint leaves and a bottle of oil. Peppermint was good for digestion—maybe that would help to settle the dragon's stomach.

"Come on, box," he said, picking it up by the two silver handles. "We've got a patient to examine." But the box lay silent in his arms. He gave it a shake. "Hey! Wake up," he said.

"We've got work to do." The box gave a small shudder, flashed blue, and opened its lid a fraction. Then, with no warning, thousands of tiny, brightly colored bugs poured out, covering it in a seething mass of feelers and tickly legs, which started to crawl up Demon's arms.

"Ugh!" he said, dropping the box hurriedly and trying to brush them off. They fell to the floor and vanished in a twinkle of tiny sparks. "What is the matter with you? What are those things?"

A muffled metallic voice came from underneath the mass of bugs. "Debugging required. Debugging required. Exiting all programs. System crash imminent." With that, it snapped shut and went still and silent. Demon stamped his foot angrily.

"WHY?" he shouted, running his hands through his hair till it stood on end. "WHY DO YOU ALWAYS GO WRONG JUST WHEN I REALLY NEED YOU?" He kicked the box so hard that it fell onto its side.

"Dear me, Pandemonius," said a voice from the doorway. "I'm not sure Hephaestus would be very pleased to see you treating his gift like that! Is there a problem?" Demon looked up and saw a tall, thin god with a mischievous smile on his face.

"Yes!" he said grumpily. "There is. I've got a depressed dragon with stinky stomach gas, and now my stupid box has decided not to work, so I can't find out what's wrong with the beast. If the goddesses smell the stinky stomach gas, I'm charcoal, and the poor beast will be sent to Tartarus. And if I don't cure it, Ares will mince up my legs and arms and make me run around his parade ground forever!" He sat down on the box with a thud and dropped his head into his hands. "I might as well ask Hera and the rest of them to sizzle me now. Then at least it would all be over."

Hermes, chief messenger of the gods, laughed. "Come on," he said, pulling Demon up. "Let's take your box to Hephaestus. He'll be able to mend it in no time. He did make it, after all."

"But what if he can't?" asked Demon.

"Then we'll think of another plan," said the god. "'Never despair,' that's my motto. There's always a solution if you look in the right place!"

CHAPTER 7

HEPHAESTUS AND HERMES

Demon trailed along behind Hermes, his heart somewhere underneath his sandals. Despite the god's cheerful words, he knew he didn't have much time. The dragon-gas smell was much worse than the problem he'd had with the Cattle of the Sun when he first arrived on Olympus. And if it built up too much in the rocky pen, he ran the risk of exploding the whole Stables—maybe even Olympus itself. He tried not to imagine what Zeus would say about that! Getting zapped by a thousand lightning bolts would be the least of it. Suddenly he skidded to an unexpected halt as a beak seized the back of his tunic with an ominous tearing sound.

"Oy! Pan's scrawny kid!" hissed the griffin, spitting out bits of cotton. "Have you asked him yet?" Demon closed his eyes and breathed hard. This was so NOT what he needed right now. But he *had* promised.

"Hermes!" he called to the god, who was now some way ahead, leaping up the path to Hephaestus's mountain as if he were a goat and singing a rude little rhyme about a nymph and a shepherd. "Could you come here a minute, please?" The god turned and made his way down the path again.

"Ah, my old friend Griffin. And how are you on this fine sunny day? Bitten anyone good lately?" Demon cleared his throat.

"Well, he thinks you owe him some nice big juicy steaks, Your Goddishness," he said. "After the

Autolykos thing." Hermes frowned.

"What Autolykos thing? What's the little scamp been up to now?" He peered around. "That reminds me. Where is he? I thought he was supposed to be helping out in the Stables."

"Well, I-I kind of threw him down the Iris Express," said Demon a bit nervously. Hermes was a friendly god, and he'd always been kind to Demon, but, as Demon had learned the hard way, gods could change from nice to nasty in the blink of a griffin's eye. "He . . . he was stealing winged-horse feathers, a-and hitting all my beasts with a broom. And he left the Stables in a horrible mess, too!"

"Oh dear," said Hermes, luckily not seeming at all upset. "Well, he was the best I could do on short notice. I did warn you he's not very trustworthy. Did you get the feathers back?" Demon nodded. "Well, I'll have a stern word with him anyway when I see him next." The god looked at the griffin, puzzled. "Why do I owe you steak, though, Griffin?"

"Me and the Nemean Lion were doing a good job of looking after the Stables till your boy came along," muttered the griffin. "Demon promised us meat if we did it properly, but then Autolykos messed it all up for us. So I reckon you owe us at least a year's worth of steak." It looked at him in a calculating way, its orange eyes sly and cunning, and clacked its beak hungrily.

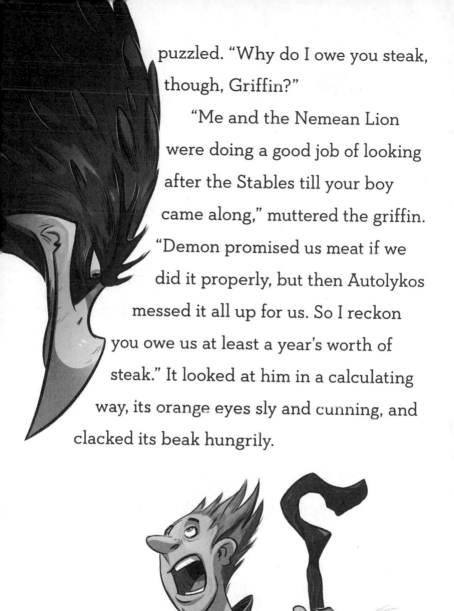

"Hmm!" Hermes said, narrowing his sky-blue eyes and tapping one finger against his snake staff. "A year's worth of steak, eh? Are you sure you and that lion were doing such a good job? Don't I remember seeing a giant scorpion heading toward Zeus's palace? Didn't I have to help you get it back in its pen?"

"Thatwasjustamistake," mumbled the griffin, looking a bit embarrassed. Demon's mouth fell open. The giant scorpion had escaped? And no one had thought he ought to know about that?

"You can have a day's worth of steaks the next time the gods have a feast," Hermes told him. "And that's the deal. Now, off to the Stables with you, cheeky beastling. Pandemonius and I have work to do."

"I'm sorry he bothered you," said Demon apologetically as the griffin flew off with a clatter of golden wings. "I didn't know about the giant scorpion."

"Don't worry about it," said Hermes. "I don't mind getting him a steak or two to keep him happy. We all get fed up with ambrosia sometimes, though don't tell Hestia I said so."

The sun was setting in a blaze of red just behind Hephaestus's mountain as they arrived, and a trickle of black smoke was drifting out of the peak. Inside the forge, there was a clattering and a clanging as six of the smith god's automaton robots loaded trolleys with shields, breastplates, bits of armor, swords, and spears.

"Ho! Brother Heffy! Where are you?" Hermes yelled over the clamor. Hephaestus emerged from behind a trolley, wiping his grimy forehead with a stained spotty handkerchief.

"Here!" he boomed. "Hang on a minute. I've just got to get this load off to the Iris Express. Ares needs them for some war he's waging down in Thessaly." Demon gave a small sigh of relief as the trolleys rattled out of the cave mouth. At least if Ares was still off fighting his stupid war, he wasn't going to be coming to find out if his dragon was cured or not.

"What's the problem NOW?" asked the smith god as the last trolley left and the forge quieted to a low hum of crackling flame and bubbling metal. Demon held out the silver box.

"I think it's broken," he said. "There were all these insect things crawling out of it, and then it went dead."

"That doesn't sound good. Did it say anything?" asked Hephaestus. Demon repeated the strange words as best he could.

"Well, that's ALL I need," said the god grouchily. "A system debug. It means taking the whole box apart with tweezers and making sure the bugs haven't bred in the programs. I'm very busy right now—Zeus wants to give Hera a new necklace to wear to a wedding, and he insists on a jewel none of the other goddesses have." He scratched his head. "I can't do it for at least a week, maybe more."

Demon felt as if he'd been punched in the gut. He'd never keep the dragon gas under control for a whole week. He let out a huge groan as Hermes bent toward him.

"Leave it to me," he whispered in Demon's ear. He stepped forward and slung an arm around Hephaestus's broad shoulders.

"Can't you really do it any sooner, Heffy? Zeus may be a bit mad if he doesn't get Hera's necklace, but if the other goddesses smell what Demon's hiding in the Stables, then I don't like to think what will happen. Remember how they treated little Eros when he set off a stink bomb at one of the feasts? And he's a god! It would be much worse for Pandemonius."

Hephaestus shuddered. "Yes, I do remember.

Poor Eros—he had to go into hiding for weeks till his feathers grew back. What wretched beast have you rescued now, Pandemonius?" he asked, looking at Demon.

As Demon explained about the stinky dragon and its gas problem, Hermes noticed something sparkly caught in Demon's sandal straps.

"Hold still a minute!" said the god. Bending down, he wiggled the sparkly thing loose and held it up to the light. Red and orange spots shimmered and danced over the cave walls.

"What in Zeus's name is that?" asked Hephaestus eagerly. He pulled the jewel out of Hermes's fingers and turned it over, examining it closely.

"Oh," Demon said. "It's one of the stinky dragon's fire jewels. It makes them when it cries. There are loads of them all over the floor of its pen."

"I'll make you a deal," said Hephaestus, seizing a piece of charcoal and starting to draw jewelry ideas on a slate with a manic gleam in his eyes. "If you bring me every one of that beastie's tears, I'll get the box back to you as soon as I can. These things are just perfect for Hera's new necklace. I've never seen anything like them! Can you keep it penned in that back cave just a bit longer?"

"Well, I suppose so," said Demon doubtfully. "But . . ." Hephaestus clapped him on the back and then turned to fiddle with something on a nearby shelf, his clever fingers working fast.

"That's the spirit. Off you go now, Pandemonius. And put this on while you're around the dragon! It should help." He handed Demon a dusty black face mask and started shouting for his automatons to bring him gold and silver as he shooed Demon and Hermes out of the cave.

"There," said Hermes as they made their way

back down the mountain. "I told you there was always a solution!"

———————◆———————

Demon wasn't so sure as he carted a load of ambrosia cake mixed with peppermint leaves into the dragon's new home. He was now wearing the charcoal-filled mask that Hephaestus had given him to help him breathe, but the smell still just about knocked him over. He closed the doors quickly behind him to keep in the stink.

"Hello," he said as cheerfully as he could through the mask. "I've brought you something to eat. It's got nice, soothing herbs in it for your tummy." The dragon was still curled up in a red ball of misery, so Demon tipped the ambrosia cake out beside it.

"What herbs?" it asked, raising its head. "If it's peppermint, don't bother. Doesn't work. I do like it, though." It uncurled itself and sniffed at the ambrosia cake, flicking out a long forked tongue to taste it. Then it sighed mournfully. "I just knew it would be peppermint. Oh well, I suppose it's better than nothing. And at least my breath will smell better. Where's that magic box of yours, then?"

"I'm afraid it's not working. Hephaestus is mending it as fast as he can. Do you think you can manage not to . . . um . . . I mean . . ." He gestured delicately at the dragon's tail, hoping it would understand. "Just until I have it again."

"I'll try," said the dragon through a mouthful of ambrosia cake. "But it's really hard to keep it in."

"And, please, can you keep the sparks in, too?" Demon asked. "It's just . . . I don't want the whole Stables to explode." The dragon eyed him.

"All right, all right! You've made your point. No sparks, no gas. I'm not stupid, you know." It went back to munching ambrosia cake and peppermint, dribbling saliva over the floor. It was almost as messy an eater as Doris.

Once Demon had swept up all the fire jewels and taken them to Hephaestus, he put the rest of the beasts to bed. Climbing up to his loft, he sniffed carefully. No stinky gas smell yet. He crossed his fingers hopefully as he pulled the spider-silk blanket over him and went to sleep. Maybe he'd get away with it, after all.

CHAPTER 8

AN ERUPTION OF GODDESSES

Demon was woken by the sound of choking and spluttering from the beasts below.

"Stinky dragon! Stinky dragon!" they all shouted in their various beastly voices. Demon's nose was suddenly assaulted by a terrible smell.

"Oh NO!" he said, pulling his tunic straight and leaping out of bed. He raced down the stairs and through the Stables, grabbing his mask as he went. The gas in the dragon's pen rushed out in a great gushing wave as he opened the doors, and he heard a thump behind him as one of the winged horses fainted.

"What happened?" he tried to ask. But the dragon smell was so bad, he had to turn tail and run, slamming the doors behind him. Some of the beasts in the Stables were wheezing and choking horribly, and he knew he had to get the worst-affected ones out immediately. But where could he put them?

Think, Demon, think! he said to himself, trying to wipe his streaming eyes with both hands. Then he remembered the paddocks at the back of the Stables, where the winged horses sometimes grazed. "Come on!" he croaked, unlocking pens as fast as he could. "Follow me! And please try not to eat each other!" Finally he had all the beasts out except for the giant scorpion, which didn't seem to be affected, so he left it where it was. He led the conscious beasts to the paddocks and let them

in, then ran back for the winged horse who had
fainted. Lugging and tugging its heavy body into a
cleanish poo barrow, he wheeled
it away as fast as he could, limp
legs hanging over the sides
and floppy white wings
dragging across the
ground.

The scene that
met his eyes in the
paddock was
absolute chaos.

The Nemean Lion was growling ferociously as
it stalked one of the Cattle of the Sun, Medea's
dragons were in a spitting fight with the Caucasian
Eagle, and the unicorns were kicking the winged

horses. Demon wrenched his dad's pipes out of his tunic, ripped off his mask, and blew the knockout emergency series of long trills his dad had taught him. Immediately, every beast lay down and fell into a deep and unbreakable sleep—all except for Khalko and Kafto, the two bronze bulls, who were immune to his pipes, being half automaton.

"Can I trust you two to behave and not breathe any sparks?" he gasped. The smell was less strong out here, but still bad enough to make his head reel.

"We'll be good," they said. "This nice green grass is a treat after all that cake." Just as Demon was going back to the Stables to try to tackle the dragon again, he spotted what looked like a multicolored whirlwind of dust coming toward him. Before Demon knew what was happening, it had picked him up and whisked him away.

"Put me down," he yelled, batting at it uselessly. But the whirlwind only held him tighter. Within seconds it had tipped him out onto a smooth, cold surface. Demon scrambled to his feet, sick, spluttering, and furious. And then he saw three pairs of icy goddess eyes glaring at him across a sea of white marble floor. All the rage drained out of him in a whoosh, and a sense of utter panic took its place. Was the thing he had feared most about to happen? Was he about to be turned into a Demon-size heap of charcoal? He tried to scramble backward, but all his limbs seemed frozen.

"WHAT IS THAT DREADFUL STINK?" said three furious goddess voices. The combined sound was like a swarm of boiling-mad bees, like a hundred packs of howling hounds, like a thousand berserk bears. It caught Demon in a great tornado of noise and flung him back across the slippery floor, stealing all the breath from him. He landed in a limp heap by a large pillar, unable to move or think.

A long and dreadful silence fell as the three goddesses waited for him to reply. Choking and coughing, Demon fought for air, his eyes closed. Somewhere inside him, a little voice was screaming for help. He knew he was doomed to be that heap of charcoal within seconds if he didn't answer!

"Oh, by the Echidna's eyeballs," said a voice behind him. "What are you all doing, terrifying Zeus's poor stable boy like that? Here, lad. Drink this!" Demon felt a cup pressed to his lips and he gulped thirstily, opening his eyes to see Hestia, goddess of the hearth, standing beside him, a large silver ladle in her other hand.

"What's this all about?" she asked, quite

unafraid of the nasty looks her fellow goddesses were sending her from across the room.

"Have you no sense of smell, Hestia?" asked Eos, goddess of the dawn. "My best bedsheets stink to high heaven!"

"My poor dear hounds' noses will never be the same again," said Artemis, goddess of the hunt, patting the heads of two hairy, red-eared dogs that sat at her feet.

"My pretty silk nightdresses reek of cesspits," said Aphrodite, goddess of love.

"AND IT'S COMING FROM THE STABLES!" yelled the goddesses together as they pointed at Demon.

"I-I-I'm s-s-s-s-s-sorry, O G-g-goddessy G-gloriousnesses," Demon stammered out. "I-I-I'm t-t-trying t-to f-fix it as f-fast as I c-can."

"And just what is this 'it'?" asked Eos in a dangerously quiet voice. Demon closed his eyes

tightly and braced himself. There was no way he
could avoid telling them.

"The-the-the C-Colchian D-D-Dragon's
s-stomach g-gas," he whispered.

"THE COLCHIAN DRAGON?" Artemis shouted angrily. "But we banished that revolting beast from Olympus years ago! Why have you brought it back?" Demon cowered as she reached for her silver bow and nocked an arrow to the string in one swift movement. Artemis never missed a shot.

"Now, now, Artemis dear, put the bow away. I'm sure there's a sensible explanation," said Hestia soothingly.

"There'd better be," growled the huntress. But she lowered the arrow so it was pointing at the ground.

"A-A-Ares commanded me to bring it to the S-Stables and cure it, Your A-amazing A-accurateness," Demon told her. "A-and th-then it a-all w-went a b-bit wrong." Artemis frowned, but Aphrodite let out a tinkling laugh. The sound was like a waterfall of warm honey, smooth and sweet and delicious.

"A bit wrong?" She giggled. "The whole of

Olympus smells like a mixture of sulfurous sewers, unwashed ancient socks, and rotten eggs, and you call it 'a bit wrong'?" She leaned back and fanned herself with a bunch of pink ostrich feathers as Demon blushed.

"W-well," he said cautiously, "m-maybe a whole lot wrong would be a b-better w-way of p-putting it, Y-your B-beauteous B-bountifulness."

Eos sighed. "I suppose if that numbskull Ares commanded you, it's not really your fault," she said. "All he ever thinks about is his wretched wars. But what are you going to do about it, Pandemonius? None of us can go outside, the nymphs have all had to lie down, the flowers are wilting, the dryads have fled down to earth, and the naiads have all disappeared underwater."

"Ah! I wondered why no one but the fauns came into the kitchen for breakfast this morning," said Hestia. "If the Colchian Dragon's here again, that would explain why. The kitchen crew and I haven't been able to smell anything since our chili powder experiments exploded yesterday morning, so the smell hasn't bothered us." She looked down at Demon. "Why haven't you used that box of yours on the beast, though? I thought it was supposed to cure everything."

"It is, Your Celestial Chefness," said Demon glumly. "But it's broken, and Hephaestus can't mend it till he's made a necklace for Zeus to give to Queen Hera." He looked around nervously, hoping the Queen of the Gods wouldn't pop out suddenly from behind a pillar. If Eos, Artemis, and Aphrodite were scary, Hera was bone-crumblingly terrifying.

"You're lucky, Pandemonius," Aphrodite said, winking at him. "Heavenly Hera's not on Olympus. She and Zeus are having a little private vacation together to make up after their last argument. They won't be back for a few days." She leaned over toward the other goddesses. "The Io episode, you know!" she hissed behind her hand.

"Just as well for you, stable boy," said Artemis, slinging her bow again and sliding the silver arrow into her quiver. "But if you don't find a cure for that smell quickly, you'll find I can be just as fierce as Hera—and believe me, I'll set my hounds to tear you apart if you fail. I'm off down to earth to wrestle a few wolves. At least it doesn't stink in the woods. Come on, girls!" She whistled to her dogs and strode out of the room.

"I must go, too," said Eos. "It's time I fed my poor Tithonus. He likes a grain or two of corn for his breakfast, and he'll only take them from my hand." She shook a finger at Demon. "Cure that beast of his smelly problem, stable boy, or I'll hang you up by the ears on my washing line for a year."

Aphrodite waited till the dawn goddess had gone, and then she chuckled. "Poor Eos! Imagine having a grasshopper for a husband. That'll teach her to ask Zeus for a favor when he's in a bad mood!" She glided over and took Demon's hand. Close up, she smelled of roses and lily of the valley, with a hint of orange blossom. Demon breathed in deeply, then felt his head spin and his knees grow weak. It wasn't wise to get too close to the goddess of love, even if the nice smell did mask the stink of dragon a bit.

"Come on, Pandemonius," she purred in her silky voice. "We'll go and see if that grimy husband of mine can't be persuaded to hurry up with your box. I'll take you to his forge by my secret underground passage. That way, we can avoid going outside." Then she gave him a sideways smile and another wink. "You can tell me all about that pretty Nereid Eunice on the way."

Demon blushed. How did Aphrodite know about Eunice?

"Don't be so nosy, Affy," Hestia said, pointing her silver ladle at the other goddess. "You know boys don't like talking about all that lovey-dovey stuff!" She ruffled Demon's hair. "Come and see me in the kitchens soon, Pandemonius. I'll be making a new batch of those honey cakes you tested out for me soon. Zeus and Dionysus can't get enough of them!"

CHAPTER 9

THE CENTAUR HEALER

As she dragged Demon through a rocky passage deep underneath Olympus, Aphrodite kept up a steady stream of gossip and inquisitive chat. She asked him a whole load of snoopy questions about Eunice and the other Nereid girls he'd met down in Poseidon's watery realm. By the time they entered Hephaestus's apartments at the back of the forge, Demon was redder than an overripe cherry.

"Oh, Heffy, darling!" cooed the goddess down a silver tube that hung coiled up by the door.

"Where are you? Your lovely Affy wants to talk to you!" Within a few minutes, there was a sound of harrumphing and stamping, and Hephaestus came in dripping with water and trying to wipe both his face and his hands clean at the same time. Seeing Demon, he stopped dead.

"What are you doing here, Pandemonius?" he asked, frowning. "How did you get into my private rooms?" Aphrodite glided forward and laid a soft white hand on his arm.

"Don't frown, Heffy dearest," she said. "It makes you all wrinkly. I brought him. You know how I hate nasty, stinky stinks, and that awful beast of Ares's is making all our lives a misery. Pandemonius really does need that magic box to cure it. You're so clever, I know you can mend it in a trice, and then everything can go back to smelling normal again." She threw herself at Hephaestus and covered his beard with kisses. Demon's face was now verging on purple with embarrassment. Hephaestus himself was spluttering and looking most uncomfortable as she wormed her way under his arm and looked up at him expectantly through her long eyelashes.

"The thing is, my dear," he said, harrumphing loudly, "you know I'd do anything for you, but the box is damaged worse than I thought. The bugs have eaten away all the workings inside, and there's one magical part in there that took me weeks to make. I'll be as quick as I can, but I can't promise anything. Pandemonius will just have to try to find another way to cure the dragon's stinking stomach." He glanced over at Demon. "Have you tried peppermint on it?"

Demon nodded. "It doesn't work," he said. Aphrodite stamped one tiny foot and burst into tears. If possible, she looked even more beautiful when she was crying.

"I can't bear it," she said, wriggling out from

under Hephaestus's arm. "I won't have it!" She stamped her foot again, and a flock of cross-looking turtledoves erupted from the floor and flew around Demon's and Hephaestus's heads, pecking them and beating them with their wings. "FIX IT!"

she shouted, pointing a finger at Demon as she flounced out. "Or I'll turn you into a myrrh tree and chop you down to make arrows for Eros!"

"Oh dear," said Hephaestus, fending off beaks and claws. "She will, too, Demon. You'd better cure that dragon or you'll end up as kindling."

"But I don't know how!" Demon wailed. "And the smell's so bad, I can't get near it, even with your mask!"

"I think," said Hephaestus, scratching his grimy beard thoughtfully so that flakes of charcoal and ash fell onto his leather apron, "it's time to call in the heavy cavalry. We need Chiron the centaur. I'll send you down to Mount Pelion to get him." He looked serious. "Chiron's your only hope. He's Zeus's brother, and a god in his own right, but the two of them don't get along too well sometimes. He'll take some persuading to come up here—and I don't know if even he can sort this mess out! Come on, we need to hurry! I still have to finish that necklace for Zeus!" He flung open the door and strode into the forge, with Demon hard on his heels. "Keep the fires low," he roared at the automaton robots as he marched past them. "And keep the fans going. We don't want any of that dragon gas building up in here! I'll be back in a minute." Reaching out to his workbench, he snagged two masks and tossed one at Demon. "Put that on. It's a better prototype than the one I made you yesterday." He took a deep breath, clapped his own mask over his beard, and left the forge at a run, Demon at his heels.

"IRIS!" he bellowed. "URGENT DELIVERY FOR MOUNT PELION!" The rainbow whooshed into sight immediately. "Take Pandemonius to Chiron's cave, quick as you can," he said. With that, he turned on his heel and raced back to his forge. "Good luck," he yelled over his shoulder.

The Iris Express dumped Demon on the very top of a mountain. It had groves of silvery wild olive growing on its steep flanks, and in the distance, Demon could see the blue-purple shimmer of the sea. As Iris's rainbow faded back into the sky, a huge creature trotted out of a nearby cave. He had a bright chestnut horse's body, but his bearded face and hairy torso were that of a man. He smelled like sweet herbs and wild places, and he had kind deep-blue eyes that looked right into Demon. This had to be Chiron.

"Please, Your Great Healeryness," he said, dropping to his knees at the centaur god's front hooves. "You've got to help me."

"Whoa! Whoa!" said Chiron, holding up a green-stained hand. "Who are you, young man? And how did you get the Iris Express to deliver you here? You're not a new god, are you?"

"Hephaestus sent me," said Demon hurriedly.

"I'm Pandemonius, son of Pan, but most people call me Demon, and I've got a sick dragon with stomach gas that is going to blow up Olympus, and the goddesses are going to hunt me down and hang me up and turn me into a tree if I don't cure it, and Ares is going to mince my legs and . . ." He ran out of words and came to a full stop, gasping for breath.

"Well, you do seem to have a problem, don't you?" said Chiron gravely, his bushy eyebrows twitching. "I think you'd better come into my cave and tell me exactly what's going on."

Inside Chiron's cave was the most amazing healing space Demon had ever seen. Shafts of natural sunlight from windows set high in the mountainside lit up shelves and shelves of neatly arranged bottles and jars filled with powdered herbs, roots, and colorful pills and potions. The drying racks mounted on the stone ceiling hung with muslin bags full of leaves, blossoms, and berries. There was a sparklingly clean operating table with gleaming rows of instruments, and a canvas hoist set to one side of it. There was a bench with pestles, mortars, and knives for chopping, and, behind a curtain, he could see another cave room with rows of neatly made empty beds piled with folded blue blankets. There were also piles and piles of open books scattered about with drawings of different sorts of human and beast anatomy as well as parts of plants and flowers. Demon stared around him in amazement. It made his hospital shed look like a joke.

"Here," said the centaur, stirring a bright red powder into what looked like purple grape juice. "Drink this. It'll give you energy and strength. I can see just from looking at you that you're carrying around a heavy burden."

Between sips of the drink, which was delectably cool and tongue-tinglingly sharp, Demon told his story again. As he did so, he could feel a delicious sense of well-being spreading over his whole body. "Hephaestus said you're my last hope," he finished.

"I see," said Chiron. One front hoof pawed the ground, and his large green-stained fingers tapped out a thoughtful rhythm on the scrubbed wooden bench. "So you want me to come up to Olympus to try to cure this beast, do you, Demon?" Demon nodded, crossing his own fingers behind his back. He badly needed some luck here.

"But what about my pupils? What about my own patients? They need me, too. I can't just leave them with no healer," the centaur said. "And I hate Olympus. Wretched place. All those gods and goddesses throwing their weight around—especially my thundery brother. I like the peace and quiet I get down here on earth."

"Oh, please," Demon begged. "I'm sure it won't take long. And Zeus is away at the moment, so you won't run into him. Don't you have anyone down here you can leave in charge?" He peered past Chiron's smooth brown shoulder into the cave with beds. "You don't seem to have any patients."

"Well . . ." The centaur god paused. "I suppose there's nothing immediately urgent in the way of patients. I sent the last one home to convalesce this morning—that silly boy Melanion got savaged by a bear.

And I suppose Asclepius could keep an eye on things and teach the apprentices. I've only got two at the moment: young Kokytos and his friend Actaeon." He looked at Demon sternly. "But I'm only coming up to Olympus for a short while, understand. Just until I've solved the dragon's stomach problem. I'm pretty sure I know what will cure it, but we'd better take several of my potions, just to be sure. Wait here while I go and make the arrangements." Calling for Asclepius, he cantered out of the cave and away through the olive groves.

Demon occupied himself by leafing through the books. He couldn't understand the funny squiggles underneath the pictures, but the drawings were amazing, and soon he was completely absorbed, his finger tracing the whorls and curlicues of the inside of a snake's ear, and then the way a set of bean seeds fitted exactly inside their fuzzy pod. There was just so much he didn't know!

When Chiron came back a short while later, he grabbed a green gauze bag and handed it to Demon, who was almost dancing with relief that Chiron had agreed to help him. "Watch and learn, young Demon," he said, picking out a whole array of bottles, ointments, and powders and putting them in the bag Demon was holding. Stretching up for a bunch of bright blue berries with one hand, he reached for protective masks and wintergreen-soaked nose plugs with the other. "If you're going to do the job properly, you can't always rely on that magical contraption of Hephaestus's to come up with answers for you. You need to learn how to cure those beasts in the Stables by yourself. I see you're interested in those books I've got. I've a good mind to ask that thundery brother of mine to let you come down here once a week so I can teach you the basics of good healing. Would you like that?"

"Oh yes, please! I WOULD!" said Demon, a big grin exploding onto his face. He hadn't actually known it till this exact minute, but having a real healing teacher was just what he really wanted.

CHAPTER 10

THE APPRENTICE HEALER

Armed with thick surgical masks and nose plugs, Demon and Chiron climbed aboard the Iris Express. It was just as well they were prepared, because when they arrived on Olympus, there was a dreadful greenish haze over the whole place, and it looked completely deserted. Clearly everyone was huddling inside the palaces with the windows sealed tightly, trying to keep away from the smell. The flowers were drooping terribly, and the trees were shedding leaves at a rapid rate. Even the wintergreen-soaked nose plugs didn't keep out the stink entirely.

"Iris," said Chiron in a muffled voice. "Go and fetch Boreas, please. Tell him it's urgent, and that he must bring his strongest bag of winds. We'll need him to blow this gas cloud away into the heavens, or the whole place will go up at the first spark." Demon had never seen the Iris Express leave so fast. Clearly the rainbow messenger didn't want to linger anywhere near Olympus, either, and he didn't blame her.

"Take me to your dragon," said Chiron. "And get on my back—it'll be faster." Chiron kneeled down so that Demon could climb on, and rather gingerly he clambered onto the broad horse's back. It felt odd and rather irreverent to be riding a god! With a lurch, the centaur god got to his hooves and took off at a straight gallop, glass bottles clinking dangerously against one another in the green bag.

Demon held on with his legs and flung his arms around Chiron's muscley waist. He just had time to think that riding a centaur was quite different from riding Keith the winged horse, and then they were hurtling past the giant scorpion and pulling up at the doors of the dragon pen.

"Careful does it," said Chiron, opening them a crack. A thick cloud of deep green fog billowed out as they entered, too thick to see through, so they retreated outside again. "It's no good," the centaur said. "We need to wait for Boreas to blow it all away. Let's wait outside. He shouldn't be long." Demon said nothing. He couldn't. He was too busy trying not to faint, taking tiny, shallow breaths through his mask and worrying about the dragon. No wonder the poor beast was in a worse state than ever, what with people slamming doors on him and running away all the time.

Suddenly Demon shivered, ducking as a spatter

of hailstones fell out of the sky, stinging his bare
arms and shoulders with their coldness.

"Here he comes," said Chiron, pointing upward.
Suddenly the green haze scattered, and against the
clear blue sky, Demon saw a stallion made of wispy
white clouds and, on its back, a purple-winged god
with curly snow-white hair and a beard stiff with
frost.

"Ho! Chiron! What can I do for you? Iris said it was urgent," said the god of the North Wind, leaping off the cloud horse. He fanned a purple wing in front of his face. "*Faugh!* What a stink! No wonder you're wearing those mask things."

"Yes, it's terrible, isn't it?" said Chiron. "Young Demon here has a dragon with a badly upset stomach. We need you to unleash your winds and blow the gas away quickly so that we can get to it and begin treatment." The wind god laughed.

"No sooner said than done," he said. "Two strings will do it, I think. Hold on to your hats, boys!" Unhitching a stout leather bag as round as a bubble from his belt, he unfastened two of the strings at its neck, one red, one black. Immediately two enormous gusts of wind burst out. Each had a merry face with puffed-out cheeks.

"Command us, O Master of Storms!" they said.

"Blow, my winds, blow!" cried Boreas. "Take

every trace of this stinky beast's stench and scatter it to the heavens!" The winds obeyed, blasting themselves all over Olympus in a second, entering every nook and cranny where the gas lurked, whisking stray straws, fallen leaves, dust, grass, hair, feathers, petals, and one of Aphrodite's silk nighties up, up, up, into the clean air above. Gathering all the gas into a whirling green cone, they sucked it up high into the sky, right over Hephaestus's mountain. Suddenly, as one stray spark drifted up from the rocky chimney and hit the cone, there was a huge bang and a flash of green and violet flame. Everything in Olympus rocked on its foundations, and then the gas was all gone.

"Thank you, Boreas," cried Chiron as the wind god waved farewell and galloped off into the heavens. "Now, quickly, Demon. We must get to the dragon before it has a chance to start up again." Demon ran to the dragon-pen doors and flung them wide.

The dragon was sprawled all over the floor of the back pen in a mass of quivering red serpentine coils. Its flame-like eyes were revolving in its head, and it was repeating *"mustholditin-mustholditin-mustholditin"* in a high, scared mumble as it shivered and shook in a kind of petrified trance.

"Right," said Chiron, entering with a clatter of hooves. "Get it to down these immediately. Three spoons of each." He handed Demon three bottles— one orange, one yellow, and one a virulent bright green—and a small golden ladle.

Carefully setting the bottles down on the floor, Demon awkwardly wedged the dragon's jaws open with one arm, risking a bite from the long, sharp teeth. "One. Two. Three," he counted over and over again, as nine ladlesful of medicine slid down its gullet. He and Chiron waited anxiously as long minutes ticked by and there was no response from the beast. It continued to shiver, shake, and mutter intermittently.

"Never mind," said Chiron, holding out a large, sticky, strong-smelling ball of blue goop, which he'd been mashing between his hands while they waited. "Let's give it one of these. It's my patented remedy for stubborn stomach-gas cases. If this doesn't work, then nothing will. Stuff it right down as far as it will go. Here, I'll hold those jaws apart for you." The centaur went down on his front legs, then folded his horse haunches underneath him, reaching out with sticky hands to draw the dragon's jaws wide open. Demon took the squishy, slippery mass and pushed it deep inside the dragon's throat till his arm had disappeared up to the shoulder. Suddenly, the dragon swallowed, and Demon felt his fingers begin to burn as a sudden spray of sparks popped upward.

"Ouch!" he yelled, whipping his scorched arm out and shaking it frantically, as the dragon began coughing out gobbets of pale purple-blue fire, sending more sparks whizzing around the cave.

"Here," said Chiron absentmindedly, his eyes fixed on the beast, which was now gulping and gargling ominously, as if it was going to be sick.

Reaching into the green bag and pulling out a pot of pale-blue ointment, he waved it in Demon's direction. "Dip your fingers in this."

Just as a blissful coolness was washing over Demon's burned bits, the dragon gave a loud belch, which smelled strongly of ginger. "That's it, old boy," said the centaur, stroking its horns. "Let it all out. You'll soon be right as rain."

Three enormous burps later, Chiron let out a big sigh of relief. "That's what I wanted to hear," he said. "It should be fine now. I'll show you how to mix up my remedy before I leave. If you give it a dose four times a day for the next month, it should be cured. But it must stay on Olympus till the course of medicine is finished, and you'll have to keep it warm and make sure its mind is occupied so it doesn't fall into an anxious state again. I can see from the condition of its scales that it's been eating completely the wrong diet. It shouldn't be a red dragon at all—its natural color is purple. It needs to eat plenty of charcoal and have regular doses of fennel seeds and ginger on its ambrosia cake."

The dragon was looking perkier by the minute. Its eyes had stopped revolving now. It shook out its coils and rattled its mane spines.

"By Ares's spear!" it said, nosing along its own body. "I haven't felt this hungry since I was a dragonling. Did someone mention charcoal? I could go for a nice, big bowl of charcoal to crunch."

"You can come with me and fetch some from Hephaestus's forge as soon as I've got the other animals back in their pens," said Demon, patting the dragon. "I'm so glad you're feeling better."

Chiron stayed with the dragon while Demon went out to the pasture. All the beasts lay scattered about the field where he'd left them, still fast asleep. Khalko and Kafto were grazing contentedly among them. He fumbled in his tunic for his pipes and put them to his lips. Blowing a soft whisper of sound into each beast's ear, he woke them one by one and led them back to their pens in the Stables. By the time he came to the griffin, whom he'd left till last, he was exhausted. The sun was high in the sky, and he'd had nothing to eat that day, and nothing to drink since Chiron's potion.

"Hello, Pan's scrawny kid," said the griffin, stretching and yawning. "Cured that stinky thing, have you? Where's my steak?" Demon laughed. Things were definitely back to normal!

As the dragon slithered up the steep path toward Hephaestus's forge, Demon suddenly had a brilliant idea.

"Are you there, Heffy?" he called. "I've brought you a visitor." Hephaestus appeared in the doorway of the forge, looking disheveled.

"We're not exactly prepared for visitors, young

Pandemonius," he said. "Those winds Boreas let out may have blown all the stink away, but they've also knocked over all the stuff in the forge and blown out the fire. Me and the robots have got a terrible mess to clear up, there's ruined charcoal crumbs all over the place, and I don't know how we're ever going to get the Zeus-blasted forge going again so I can finish off that necklace for Hera."

Demon beamed at him. This was going to be much easier than he'd thought. His brilliant idea might just work. "Meet the Colchian Dragon," he said, gesturing behind him. "The answer to all your problems!"

"Ah! So this is the beastie that's caused all the trouble, is it? Cured now, are you?"

"Yes," said the dragon. "And I'm STARVING!" It snapped its jaws hungrily. Hephaestus hastily backed away from the sharp teeth, then frowned.

"Well, I don't know what you want me to do

about it," he said. "I'm not a dragon restaurant. And what do you mean, it's the answer to all my problems?"

"Well, that's the interesting part," said Demon, feeling smug. "The Colchian Dragon needs a new job to keep his spirits up, at least till Ares comes back from his war. He loves charcoal, so he can eat up all the ruined stuff for you—it won't matter to him if it's a bit crumbly—and he can easily light your forge and keep it going. Chiron tells me that once he's all better, his fire will be the hottest of any dragon. Meanwhile, he needs somewhere warm to curl up while he's convalescing. You can have a real dragon on hand when the forge needs to be put in dragon mode!"

Hephaestus scratched his head. "You seem to have it all worked out," he said. "And how do you feel about it, Dragon?" But the dragon didn't answer. It had slipped past Hephaestus and was busy gobbling down charcoal bits as fast as it could crunch.

"I think he likes it here," said Demon. "I'll be back with his medicine later. He's a very nice dragon now that he doesn't smell anymore!"

"You're a scamp, young Demon," grumbled Hephaestus, stepping over the dragon's coils to go back into the forge. The tip of the dragon's arrow-shaped tail was already turning a bright royal purple. "But I suppose you've got a good heart."

Demon met Chiron back at the Stables, where the centaur god had just checked out all the beasts to make sure they hadn't come to any harm from being asleep for so long. They were fine, but hungry, so Demon quickly filled the mangers with ambrosia cake. Then he and the centaur went over to the hospital shed.

"Not bad," said Chiron, looking around

approvingly. "Clean, neat, and tidy. That's what I like to see." Demon blushed.

"I've got so much to learn, though, if I'm going to manage without the box," he said. Chiron reached into his green gauze bag and started pulling out ingredients.

"Then let's start right here, young apprentice healer," he said. "No time like the present."

Demon sighed happily. Apprentice healer. He liked the sound of that title VERY much!

GLOSSARY

PRONUNCIATION GUIDE

THE GODS

Aphrodite (AF-ruh-DY-tee): Goddess of love and beauty and all things pink and fluffy.

Ares (AIR-eez): God of war. Loves any excuse to pick a fight.

Artemis (AR-te-miss): Goddess of the hunt. Can't decide if she wants to protect animals or kill them.

Boreas (BOR-ee-us): The blustery god of the North Wind and winter.

Dionysus (DY-uh-NY-suss): God of wine. Turns even sensible gods into silly goons.

Eos (EE-oss): The Titan goddess of the dawn. Makes things rosy with a simple touch of her fingers.

Eris (AIR-iss): Ares's sister, the goddess of chaos. Loves stirring up trouble as much as her brother does.

Eros (AIR-oss): The rascally, winged god of love.

Hades (HAY-deez): Zeus's brother and the gloomy, fearsome ruler of the Underworld.

Hephaestus (Hih-FESS-tuss): God of blacksmithing, metalworking, fire, volcanoes, and most things awesome.

Hera (HEER-a): Zeus's scary wife. Drives a chariot pulled by screechy peacocks.

Hermes (HUR-meez): The clever, fun-loving, jack-of-all-trades messenger god.

Hestia (HESS-tee-ah): Goddess of the hearth and home. Bakes the most heavenly treats.

Pan (PAN): God of shepherds and flocks. Frequently found wandering grassy hillsides, playing his pipes.

Poseidon (puh-SY-dun): God of the sea and controller of natural and supernatural events.

Zeus (ZOOSS): King of the gods. Fond of smiting people with lightning bolts.

OTHER MYTHICAL BEINGS

Autolykos (ow-TOL-ih-kohs): A trickster who shape-shifts his stolen goods to avoid getting caught.

Chiron (KY-ron): A super centaur, and the oldest. Known for his wisdom and healing abilities.

Dryads (DRY-ads): Tree nymphs. Can literally sing trees to life.

Heracles (HAIR-a-kleez): The half-god "hero" who just *loooves* killing magical beasts.

Jason: Another pesky "hero" who will hurt any beast that stands in the way of a quest.

Medea (mih-DEE-ah): A witch princess from Colchis who helped the hero Jason (for some reason).

Naiads (NYE-adz): Freshwater nymphs—keeping Olympus clean and refreshed since 500 BC.

Nereids (NEER-ee-idz): A sisterhood of fifty sea nymphs who love to gossip.

Nymphs (NIMFS): Giggly, girly, dancing nature spirits.

PLACES

Colchis (KOL-kiss): An ancient kingdom on the Black Sea where Jason brought his ship of heroes.

Mount Pelion (PEEL-ee-un): A mountain on the Aegean Sea where Chiron the centaur lives.

Tartarus (TAR-ta-russ): A delightful torture dungeon miles below the Underworld.

BEASTS

Centaur (SEN-tor): Half man, half horse, and lucky enough to get the best parts of both.

Colchian Dragon (KOL-kee-un): Ares's guard dragon. Has magical teeth and *supposedly* never sleeps.

Cretan Bull (KREE-tun): A furious, fire-breathing bull. Don't stand too close.

Griffin (GRIH-fin): Couldn't decide if it was better to be a lion or an eagle, so decided to be both.

Hydra (HY-druh): Nine-headed water serpent. Hera somehow finds this lovable.

Khalkotauroi (KALL-koh-tor-OY): Khalko and Kafto, Hephaestus's fire-breathing, half-automaton bronze bulls.

Nemean Lion (NEE-mee-un): A giant, indestructible lion. Swords and arrows bounce off of his fur.

ABOUT THE AUTHOR

Lucy Coats studied English and ancient history at Edinburgh University, then worked in children's publishing, and now writes full-time. She is a gifted children's poet and writes for all ages from two to teenage. She is widely respected for her lively retellings of myths. Her twelve-book series Greek Beasts and Heroes was published by Orion in the UK. Beasts of Olympus is her first US chapter-book series. Lucy's website is www.lucycoats.com. You can also follow her on Twitter @lucycoats.

ABOUT THE ILLUSTRATOR

As a kid, **Brett Bean** made stuff up to get out of trouble. As an adult, Brett makes stuff up to make people happy. Brett creates art for film, TV, games, books, and toys. He works on his tan and artwork in California with his wife, Julie Anne, and son, Finnegan Hobbes. He hopes to leave the world a little bit better for having him. You can find more about him and his artwork at www.2dbean.com.